Joseph Williamson Randolph

The Letter Writer

Or, the art of polite correspondence : containing a variety of plain and

elegant letters on business, love, courtship, marriage, relationship,

friendship, &c

Joseph Williamson Randolph

The Letter Writer
Or, the art of polite correspondence : containing a variety of plain and elegant letters on business, love, courtship, marriage, relationship, friendship, &c

ISBN/EAN: 9783337386290

Printed in Europe, USA, Canada, Australia, Japan

Cover: Foto ©Andreas Hilbeck / pixelio.de

More available books at **www.hansebooks.com**

THE

LETTER WRITER,

OR, THE ART OF

POLITE CORRESPONDENCE.

CONTAINING A VARIETY OF

PLAIN AND ELEGANT LETTERS

ON

BUSINESS, LOVE, COURTSHIP, MARRIAGE,

RELATIONSHIP, FRIENDSHIP, &c.

SECOND EDITION.

J. W. RANDOLPH,
121 MAIN ST., RICHMOND, VA.
1863.

MACFARLANE & FERGUSSON, PRINTERS.

CONTENTS.

ON BUSINESS

ON FRIENDSHIP.

THE
LETTER WRITER.

ON BUSINESS.

LETTER 1.

From a Young Tradesman to Wholesale Dealers, with an Order.

GENTLEMEN,

I hope it will not be a disagreeable surprise to see below an order on my account.

I am not in the least doubtful of your serving me on the best terms; that is, so as to enable me to sell as cheap as others. And whenever you have occasion for money, your demand shall either be paid, or you may draw on me for the amount. Pray be careful in choosing my goods, and expeditious in forwarding them, which will tend to increase your correspondence with,

Gentlemen,

Your most obedient servant.

LETTER 2.

From a Young Man whose Master had lately died.

SIR,

I doubt not but you have heard of my late worthy master's death. I have served him as an apprentice and journeyman above twelve years; and as his widow does not choose to carry on the business, I have taken the store and stock in trade, and shall be glad to deal with you in the same manner he did. I have sent the enclosed order for payment of such bills as are due, and you may depend on punctuality with respect to the remainder, for which purpose let them be entered as my debt. Please to send the enclosed order, and let the goods be the best you have, which will oblige

Your humble servant.

LETTER 3.

The Answer.

SIR,

Yours I received, and am extremely sorry to hear of the death of my good friend, your late master; but, at the same time, pleased that his business has fallen into such good hands as yours. You have double advantage over a stranger, as you are well acquainted both with your late master's trade and customers, which, by his dealings with me appear to be very extensive. I have sent your order in ten bales, marked O. P., by the Speedwell, of Norfolk, John Thompson, master, and you will find them as good and cheap as any that are to be had in the city. I heartily thank you for your offered correspondence; and shall, on all occasions, use you with honor.

I wish you all manner of success; and am

Your humble servant.

LETTER 4.

From a Tradesman to a Customer, demanding Payment of Money.

SIR,

Your bill for goods supplied last year has now been delivered upwards of three months, and I have waited on you several times to solicit payment, but have not been so fortunate as to find you at home. I have a very large sum to make up in the course of a week and shall esteem it a very particular favor, if you can let me have the amount of my bill delivered within that time. I trust you will excuse the liberty I take in writing to you on this subject, and believe me, sir,

Your most obedient, humble servant.

LETTER 5.

Answer to the Preceding.

SIR,

I am sorry you have had the trouble of calling so often for your money, and still more that it is not in my power to pay your bill within the time you mention; I am at present very short of cash, and shall be so for six weeks; at the end of that time I will settle with you.

1 am, sir; your humble servant.

LETTER 6.

The Tradesman's Reply.

SIR,

I should be sorry to appear troublesome to any customer; but you, who are not in any business, may not probably know how subject tradesmen are to large demands for cash, and how much an omission of payment may injure them in the world. The credit on your bill already exceeds, by some months, what it is usual in trade to give, and what I give my customers in general; I hope, therefore, you will not take it amiss, that I have drawn on you at six weeks for the amount of my demand. I have sent the bill by my clerk for your acceptance, not doubting that it will be duly honored, and that you will excuse this liberty from,

Sir, your most obedient,
Humble servant.

LETTER 7.

From a Tradesman unable to honor his acceptance, to a Merchant.

DEAR SIR,

It gives me the greatest pain to be under the necessity of writing to you on the subject I am now about to do; but I think it better to apprize you of the circumstances beforehand, than to permit a bill with your name on it to be dishonored without your knowledge. The failure of Mr. C., who was my debtor to a considerable amount, and from whom I was in daily expectation of payment, has strained me for cash so much, that I can only raise $30 towards the amount of the bill for $97 17, which I accepted in your favor, and which will become due the day after to-morrow.

If you would have the kindness, if the bill remains in

your hands, to receive that sum in part, and my acceptance at two months for the remainder, I will take care it
shall be duly attended to; or if the bill is out of your
hands, if you would favor me with cash to supply the de-
ficiency, I will give you the like bill, and allow discount,
with pleasure. I am given to understand there will be a
considerable dividend of Mr. C.'s effects: if an assign-
ment of my claim on him would be any satisfaction to
you, as a collateral security, I am willing to make it, or
to do anything else in my power to convince you that I
mean to act honestly. I am, dear sir,

Your sincere friend,

And obliged humble servant.

LETTER 8.

From a Tenant to a Landlord, excusing delay of Payment.

Sir,

I have been your tenant above ten years in the house
where I now live, and you know that I have never failed
to pay my rent quarterly when due. At present I am extremely sorry to inform you, that from a variety of losses
and disappointments, I am under the necessity of begging
that you will indulge me one quarter longer; by that time
I hope to have it in my power to answer your just demand,
and the favour shall be ever gratefully acknowledged by
your

Obedient, humble servant.

LETTER 9.

The Answer.

SIR,

It was never my design to oppress you. I have had long trial of your honesty, and therefore you may rest perfectly satisfied concerning your present request. No demand shall be made by me, upon you for rent, until it suits you to pay it; for I am convinced you will not keep it from me any longer.

I am, yours sincerely.

LETTER 10,

An urgent demand of Payment.

SIR,

The exigence of my affairs compels me thus importunately, nay, peremptorily to write to you. Can you think it possible to carry on business in the manner you act by me? You know what promises you have made, and how, from time to time, you have broken them. Can I, therefore, depend upon any new ones you make? If you use others as you do me, how can you think of carrying on business? If you do not, what must I think of the man who deals worse by me than he does by others? If you think you can trespass more upon me than you can on others, that is a very bad compliment to my prudence, or your own gratitude; for surely good usage should be entitled to the same in return. I know how to allow for disappointments as well as any man; but can a man be disappointed forever? Trade is so dependent a thing that it cannot be carried on without mutual punctuality. Does not the merchant expect it from me for those very goods I send you? And, can I make a return to him without receiving it from you? What end can it answer to give you two years' credit, and then be at an uncertainty, for goods which I sell at a small profit, and have only six months' credit for myself? Indeed, sir, this will never do. I must be more punctually used by you, or else deal with as little punctuality with others; and then, what must be the consequence? In short, sir, I expect a handsome payment by the next return, and security for the remainder. I am loth to take any harsh measures to procure justice to myself, my family, and creditors.

For I am, if it be not your own fault,

Your faithful friend and servant.

***

LETTER 11.

The Answer.

Sir,

I acknowledge with gratitude the lenity you have at all times shown, and my being obliged to disappoint you so often has given me much uneasiness. I do assure you, sir, that I am not so ungrateful as my conduct has given you reason to believe. From the state of my accounts you will find that the greatest part of my property is in the hands of country dealers, who, although they seldom fail, yet their times of payment are very precarious and uncertain. However, to convince you of my integrity, I have sent by this day's post an order for seventy dollars, and next week you shall receive one much larger. The remainder shall be sent in a short time. I am determined for the future to make the rules laid down in your excellent letter a guide, in my dealings with those people, whose dilatoriness in making good their payments to me, obliges me to disappoint you; and to convince you further of my integrity, the goods which I order, until the old account is paid off, shall be for ready money. I doubt not but you will continue to treat me with the same good usage as formerly, and believe me to be unfeignedly,

Your obliged,

Humble servant.

LETTER 12.

From a Merchant to a Tradesman, demanding Money, and expressing Disapprobation of his Proceedings.

SIR,

Enclosed is your account, and I am sorry the statement of your mode of living, which has been reported to me, is such, that I must in justice to myself demand an immediate payment of the balance. It is not my disposition to act unkindly, or distress any man; but when I see people with my property in their hands, squandering away their substance in wanton extravagance, it becomes necessary for me to see a little to my affairs. Sir, I am informed you keep a horse and chaise, and country lodgings; that you belong to clubs, and are a Buck of the fashion, a Free and Easy, and I know not what else: in a word, that business is but a secondary concern with you; nay, what is worse, I hear it hinted that you game. I began the world, sir, with a greater capital than you, and with as good a connection, in cheaper times, but I never kept a horse till I was not able to walk, and other men no richer than myself kept their coach. As to the sin and folly of wasting my time in debauchery and gaming, I was always above it, for whatever you may think, a man is much more credibly employed in his business, than in sotting amongst mimics and stage-players, or wasting money not his own, amongst sharpers.

Sir, your having married my kinswoman will not protect you against my taking the necessary steps to recover my money; were you my own son, I would not act otherwise, and am very sorry to have reason to cease subscribing myself,

Your sincere friend.

LETTER 13.

Soliciting the Loan of Money from a Friend.

DEAR SIR,

I believe that ever since you first knew me, you will be ready to acknowledge that no person was ever more diffident in asking favors than myself. Indeed, I have always considered it more pleasing to an honest mind, to confer, than to receive a favor: but an unexpected affliction in my family obliges me to solicit your assistance by the loan of about forty dollars for six months ; but on this condition, that you can spare it without hurting yourself; for I would by no means choose that my friend should suffer in his present circumstances in order to oblige me. Indeed, sir, I was some days engaged amongst my acquaintances to raise the money, before I could prevail with myself to ask it from you ; and that I have now done it, is from a principle far more noble than any lucrative motive; nor indeed would I have asked it at all, were I not morally certain of paying it at the time proposed. I hope this will not give any offence, and as I before said, if it is in any way inconvenient, let me beg that you will refuse it.

I am, sir,

Yours with the greatest sincerity.

LETTER 14.

The Answer.

DEAR SIR,

I could not hesitate one moment in answering your letter ; and had I known that my worthy friend had been in want of the sum mentioned, I should never have put his unaffected modesty to the blush, by suffering him to ask it: no, sir, the offer should have come from myself. However, the sum is sent by the bearer, but let me beg, if you consider me really your friend, that you will suit the payment to your own circumstances, without being confined to a particular time; and not only so, but that you will likewise command my assistance in every thing else wherein I can serve you. But lest you think me strictly formal, I have hereby given you leave to draw on me to the amount of two hundred dollars, or for any less sum, to be paid as is most suitable to your circumstances.

I am, sir, your sincere friend.

LETTER 15.

To a person who wants to borrow Money of another, without any claim but assurance.

SIR,

While I was out of town, I find you did me the favor of inquiring two or three times for me; and among my letters I found one from you, desiring the loan of fifty dollars. You must certainly have mistaken me or yourself very much, to think we were enough known to each other for such a transaction. I was twice in your company; I was delighted with your conversation, and you seemed as much pleased with mine. Should I answer the demand of every new acquaintance, I should soon want power to oblige my old friends, and even to serve myself. Surely, sir, a gentleman of your merit cannot be so little beloved as to be forced to seek new acquaintance, and to have no better friend than one of yesterday. Be this as it may, it does not at all suit my convenience to comply with your request, and therefore I must beg you to excuse,

Yours, &c.

LETTER 16.

Refusal to Lend Money.

SIR,

I am exceedingly sorry that your request comes to me at a time, when I am so pressed by my own affairs, that I cannot, with any convenience, comply with it. On any future opportunity, when I may have money to spare, I shall be ready to oblige you. I hope, sir, you will therefore excuse

Your most humble servant.

LETTER 17.

Compliance to lend Money.

SIR,

I consider myself much obliged in the request you make me. I most cheerfully comply with it, and enclose a note for the requested sum, payable at sight; and am not a little glad it is in my power to show you how much I am, sir,

Your faithful friend and servant.

LETTER 18.

From an Insolvent Debtor to his principal Creditor, requesting an investigation of his accounts, for the benefit of his Creditors.

SIR,

When I first entered upon business, I little thought that ever I should be under the necessity of writing to you on such a subject as this; but experience teaches me, that it is much better to acknowledge the state of my affairs to my creditors, than put them to the expense of commencing suits against me. To you, therefore, sir, as the person to whom I am principally indebted, do I address myself on this melancholy occasion, and must freely acknowledge that my affairs are very much perplexed. I have these ten years past endeavored to acquire something to myself, but in vain. The variety of different articles which I have been obliged to sell on credit, and the losses sustained thereby, always kept me in low circumstances; and often when I paid you money, I had none left for the support of my family. If you will be pleased to employ some prudent person to examine my books, I doubt not but you will be convinced that the whole of my conduct has been consistent with the strictest rules of honesty; and if it shall appear so to you, I must beg you will be pleased to call a meeting of my creditors, and lay it before them. I have not spent any more than was absolutely necessary for the support of my family, and every thing remaining shall be delivered up. When all this is done, I hope you will accept of it, as it is not in my power to do any more, and consider me as one whose misfortunes call for pity instead of resentment.

I am, sir,

Your most humble servant.

LETTER 19.

The Answer.

SIR,

It is with the greatest concern·that I have perused your affecting letter: and should consider myself as very cruel indeed, if I refused to comply with a request so reasonable as that made by you. I have employed a worthy person, a friend of mine, to examine your books, the result of which shall be immediately laid before the other creditors; and if it is as you represent, you need not be afraid of any harsh usage. I always considered you as a person of integrity, and am determined to devise a plan for your future support. In the mean time, I have sent a·trifle to defray your expenses, till the other affairs are settled, and am,

Your sincere well wisher.

.LETTER 20.

From a Tradesman to a Wholesale Dealer, to delay Payment of
a sum of Money. ·

SIR,

My note to you will be payable in ten days, and I am sorry to inform you, although I have considerable sums in good hands, yet none of them are due these three weeks, which is all the time I require. It is a favor I never asked of any one till this moment, and I hope for the future not to have any occasion to repeat it. I am really distressed for your answer; but as a proof of my sincerity, have sent enclosed three notes given by persons well known to yourself; and though they exceed my debt, yet I have no objection to your keeping them as security till due. Let me beg to hear from you as soon as this comes to hand, which will greatly oblige

,Your humble servant.

LETTER 21.

The Answer.

SIR,

It was extremely fortunate for you that your letter arrived the day after it was written, for I was to have paid your note away yesterday, and I could not have had an opportunity of recalling it in time to have served you. Indeed, it was imprudent not to communicate the news to me sooner, as your credit might have been greatly affected by such an unnecessary delay. However, I impute it to your unwillingness to reveal the state of your affairs, and shall keep the note in my hands till your own becomes due, and for that purpose have returned the others, not doubting but you will send me the money at the time promised,.which will greatly oblige,

Your sincere well-wisher.

LETTER 22.

Recommending a Man Servant.

SIR,

The bearer has served me with integrity and fidelity for many years, but having a desire to visit your city, he left my house about a week ago, and by a letter received from him this day, I find you are willing to employ him on my recommendation, and it is with the greatest pleasure that I comply with his request. His behavior while with me, was strictly honest, sober and diligent, and I doubt not but it will be the same with you. I have sent this enclosed in one to himself, and if you employ him, I hope he will give satisfaction.

I am, sir, your humble servant.

LETTER 23.

From a Young Tradesman in distressed circumstances, to another of age and experience.

DEAR FRIEND,

Your knowledge of the world, joined to your goodness of heart, and adorned by the most exalted piety, encourages me to seek your advice in a case of real distress. You know that I have not been full five years in business, and although the beginning promised fair, yet, alas! I have been deceived. So does the sun shine upon us in the morning; we take our pleasure in the fields for a few hours, we are overtaken by a sudden storm, and the day concludes in thunder and lightning.

To speak in plain words, the many failures which have lately taken place in the commercial world, have brought me to the brink of temporal misery: two-thirds of my property have been fraudulently taken from me. Under such unhappy circumstances, how shall I act? I have not been indolent or extravagant, but by an ill-timed and ill-placed confidence, I have been injured.

A good character is what I strove to preserve; a good conscience is what I still enjoy: but the world is often deaf to all our pretensions to integrity. No sooner are we fallen than we are trodden under foot; our misfortunes are considered as crimes; we are despised by some, hated by others, but pitied by few. Ah! sir, when shall we learn to do as we would be done by? When shall we love our neighbors as ourselves? It is a great misfortune in trade, that every failure is considered as criminal, although the person accused is often innocent. I know you have abilities to give me advice. I know you have a tender, compassionate heart, and your charity will shine with a distinguished lustre, if displayed on the present melancholy occasion; and by your advice, perhaps, my ruin may be prevented. I have sent this by my poor afflicted wife, and will wait on you as soon as I receive your orders for that purpose. In the mean time,

I am your sincere, though afflicted friend.

ON LOVE, COURTSHIP,

AND

MARRIAGE.

—

LETTER 24.

Letter from a Gentleman to a Lady, disclosing his passion.

MADAM,

Those only who have suffered them can tell the unhappy moments of hesitating uncertainty which attend the formation of a resolution to declare the sentiments of affection ; I, who have felt their greatest and most acute torments, could not, previous to my experience, have formed the remotest idea of their severity. Every one of those qualities in you which claim my admiration, increased my diffidence, by showing the great risk I run in venturing, perhaps before my affectionate assiduities have made the desired impression on your mind, to make a declaration of the ardent passion I have long since felt for you.

My family and connections are so well known to you, that I need say nothing of them. If I am disappointed of the place I hope to hold in your affections, I trust this step will not draw on me the risk of losing the friendship of yourself and family, which I value so highly, that an object less ardently desired, or really estimable, could not induce me to take a step by which it should be in any manner hazarded.

I am, madam,

Your affectionate admirer,

And sincere friend.

--- · ---

LETTER 25.

The Answer.

Sir,

I take the earliest opportunity of acknowledging the receipt of your letter, and the obligations I feel to you for the sentiments expressed in it; and assure you, that whatever may be the event of your solicitations in another quarter, the sentiments of friendship I feel, from a long acquaintance with you, will not be in any manner altered.

There are many points besides mere personal regard to be considered; these I must refer to the superior knowledge of my father and brother; and if the result of their inquiries is such as my presentiments suggest, I have no doubt my happiness will be attended to by permission to decide for myself.

At all events, I shall never cease to feel obliged by a preference in itself sufficiently flattering, and rendered still more so by the handsome manner in which it is expressed; and I hope, if my parents should see cause to decline the proposed favor of your alliance, it will not produce such

disunion between our families, as to deprive us of friends,
who possess a great portion of our esteem and regard.

I am, sir,

Your obliged and sincere friend,

And humble servant.

LETTER 26.

From a Gentleman to a young Lady of a superior fortune.

Madam,

I can no longer do so great violence to my inclinations,
and injustice to your charms and merits, as to retain within my own breast those sentiments of esteem and affection
with which you have inspired me.

I should have hazarded this discovery much sooner, but
was restrained by dread of meeting censure, for my pre-
sumption in aspiring to the possession of a lady whom
beauty, wit, and fortune, have conspired to raise so high
above my reasonable expectations.

You have judgment enough both of your own good
qualities, and the characters of those with whom you con-
verse, to make a proper estimate of my sincerity on this
occasion. I am above deceit, and have not, therefore, at
any period of our acquaintance, pretended to be a man of
greater property than I am, which conduct I hope will
tend to convince you of my general sincerity. Believe
me, my dearest A——, were our circumstances reversed,
I should hardly take to myself the credit of doing a generous action, in overlooking the consideration of wealth,

and making you an unreserved tender of my hand and fortune. I shall await your answer in a state of unpleasant impatience, and therefore rely on your humanity not to keep me long in suspense.

I am, madam,
Your most humble servant.

LETTER 27.

The Answer.

SIR,

Giving you credit, as I do, for an elevation of mind capable of the most generous sentiments, I cannot believe you guilty of the meanness of speculating on the heart of a lady, with the view to her property. Knowing your accomplished manners, and cultivated understanding, I feel the greatest obligation to you for the polite and affectionate declaration contained in your letter. In an affair of so much importance, however, I must refer myself entirely to the discretion of my father. At the same time I must caution you against feeling hurt at minute inquiries, and resolute objections, which perhaps may be made ; young people think too little of wealth, old ones, *perhaps,* too much ; but I know my father's prudence and kindness so well, as to pledge myself to abide by his final decision, whatever pain it may cost me. Yet I advise you not to despair of success, as you will find a warm and zealous advocate in

Your sincere friend and humble servant.

LETTER 28.

From a Gentleman of some fortune, who had seen a Lady in public, to her Mother.

MADAM,

I shall be very happy if you are not altogether unac-quainted with the name which is at the bottom of this letter, since that will prevent me the necessity of saying some things concerning myself, which had better be heard from others. Hoping that it may be so, I shall not trouble you on that head; but only say, that I have the honor to be of a family not mean, and not wholly without a fortune.

I was yesterday, madam, at the rehearsal at St. Paul's, and have been informed, that a lady who commanded my attention there, has the happiness to be your daughter. It is on account of that lady that I now write to you; but I am aware that you will say this is a rash and an idle man-ner of attempting an acquaintance. I have always been of opinion that nothing deserves censure which is truly honorable and undisguised. I take the freedom to tell you, madam, that I believe your daughter worthy a much better offer; but I am assured my happiness will depend upon her accepting or refusing this. In the first place, I request to know whether the lady be engaged, for I am an entire stranger; and, if she be not, I beg, that after you have informed yourself who it is that requests the honor of being introduced to her, you will do me the singular favor of letting me be answered. I am very much an enemy, madam, to the usual nonsense upon these occa-sions; but it would be injustice to myself to conclude without saying, that my mind will be very little at ease until I know how this address is received. I have the honor to be, with the greatest respect, madam,

Your very obedient and humble servant.

LETTER 29.

From a Mother to a Gentleman, who had asked permission to address her Daughter. In Answer.

SIR,

The letter which you have done me the honour to write to me, speaks you to be a gentleman and a man of sense. I am sorry to acquaint you, that after such a prepossession in your favor, I am for more than one reason desirous to decline the offer you are pleased to make towards an alliance in my family. My daughter is very dear to me; and I think she has cast an eye elsewhere; I think there is something indelicate and improper in this wild manner of engaging in an attachment, and pleading in favor of it. I wish you had known my daughter more before you spoke so much, and had met with me among our acquaintance to have mentioned it. I am convinced, sir, that I do not think more of you than I may with justice, when I confess to you that I believe you would be more than an equal match for my daughter; for though she has (and suffer me, sir, although I am her mother, to say it) great merit, her fortune, although not quite inconsiderable, is not great. You will see, sir, that I waver in my opinion on this subject; but you must attribute it to the true cause; and believe that every thing which has, be it ever so remote, a tendency to my daughter's welfare, will make me very cautious in determining. To give you my final sense, (at least what is final to me at present,) I have not a thought of asking who it is that has thus favored us, nor would advise my daughter to remember it. I thank you, sir, in her name as well as my own, for the honor you intend us, and am, sir,

Your most obedient servant.

LETTER 30.

From a Young Tradesman to a Gentleman, desiring permission to visit his Daughter.

SIR,

I flatter myself that the integrity of my intention will excuse the freedom of these few lines, whereby I am to acquaint you of the great regard and esteem I have for your daughter. I would not, sir, attempt any indirect address that should have the least appearance of inconsistency with her duty to you, and my honorable views to her, choosing by your influence, if I may approve myself to you worthy of that honor, to commend myself to her approbation. You are not insensible, sir, by the credit I have hitherto preserved in the world, of my ability, by God's blessing, to make her happy. This the rather emboldens me to request the favor of an evening's conversation with you, at your first convenience; when I will more fully explain myself, as I earnestly hope, to your satisfaction, and take my encouragement or discouragement from

rour own mouth. I am, sir, in the mean time, with great
espect and esteem,

Your most obedient, humble servant.

LETTER 31.

From the same to the Young Lady, by permission of the Father.

Miss,

I hope I shall stand excused in venturing to make
known to your honored father, the great desire I have to
be thought worthy of a relation to him by your means.
As he has not discouraged me in the hopes I have entertained, that I may possibly be not unacceptable to him,
and to all your worthy family, I propose to do myself the
honor of a visit next Monday. Though he has been so
good as to promise to introduce me, and I make no doubt
has acquainted you with it; I nevertheless give you the
trouble of these lines, that I may not appear wanting in
any outward demonstration of that inviolable respect,
with which I am, dear Miss,

Your devoted, humble servant.

LETTER 32.

From a Widow to a Young Gentleman, rejecting his suit.

Sir,

The objections I have to make to the proposal contained in your letter are but few, but they demand some
attention, and will, I believe, be rather difficult to obviate.

You are, by your account, two-and-twenty. I am, by
mine, six-and-forty. You are too young to know the
duties of a father. I have a son who is seventeen, and
consequently too old to learn the duties of. a son from one
so little senior to himself. Thus much with respect to
age. As to the little fortune I possess, I consider myself
merely trustee for my children, and will not, therefore,
impose on you, by acceding to common report,. that I am
rich. However, as you have borne a lieutenant's commis-
sion these three years, as you tell me, you may, perhaps,
have reserved out of the profits of that, a sufficient sum
to obviate every difficulty on that head.

I will press these objections no farther ; when you can
convince me that in point of age, fortune, and morals,
you are such a person as I can, without reproach, take for
a husband, and admit as a guardian to my children, I shall
cease to think, as I now candidly confess I do, that motives
far from honorable, or disinterested love, have influenced
your application. Till that happens, I must regret that
an ill-timed effort of gallantry, on your part, deprives me
of the pleasure of subscribing myself

· Your sincere friend and humble servant.

LETTER 33.

*From a Young Lady to a Gentleman that courted her, whom she
could not esteem, but was forced by her Parents to receive his
visits, and think on none else for her husband.*

SIR, ,

It is an exceedingly ill return that I make the respect
you have for me, when I acknowledge to you, though the

day of our marriage is appointed, I am incapable of loving you. You may have observed, in the long conversations we have had at those times that we were left together, that some secret hung upon my mind. I was obliged to an ambiguous behavior. I have strict commands from both my parents to receive you, and am undone forever, except you will be so kind and generous as to refuse me. Consider, sir, the misery of bestowing yourself upon one who can have no prospect of happiness but from your death. This is a confession made, perhaps, with an offensive sincerity; but that conduct is much to be preferred to a covered dislike which could not but pall all the sweets of life, by imposing on you a companion that dotes and languishes for another. I will not go so far as to say my passion for the gentleman, whose wife I am by promise, would lead me to any thing criminal against your honor. I know it is dreadful enough to a man of your sense to expect nothing but forced civilities in return for tender endearments, and cold esteem for undeserved love. If you will, on this occasion, let reason take place of passion, I doubt not but fate has in store for you some worthier object of your affection, in recompense of your goodness to the only woman that could be insensible of your merit.

I am, sir, your humble servant.

LETTER 34.

From a Young Lady in the Country to her Father, acquainting him with an offer of Marriage.

HONORED FATHER,

My duty teaches me to acquaint you, that a gentle-

man of this town, whose name is S., and by business a
merchant, has made some overtures to my cousin A., in
the way of courtship to me. My cousin has brought him
once or twice into my company, as he has a high opinion
of him and his circumstances. He has been set up three
years, possesses a very good business, and lives in credit
and fashion. He is about twenty-seven years old, and is
likely in his person. He seems not to want sense nor
manners, and is come of a good family. He has broken
his mind to me and boasts how well he can maintain me;
but I assure you, sir, I have given him no encouragement,
yet he resolves to persevere, and pretends extraordinary
affection and esteem. I would not, sir, by any means,
omit to acquaint you with the beginning of an affair, that
would show a disobedience unworthy of your kind indul-
gence and affection. Pray give my humble duty to my
honored mother, love to my brother and sister, and respect to all friends.

       I remain your ever dutiful daughter.

LETTER 35.

The Answer.

DEAR POLLY,

     I have received your letter of the first instant, rela-
ting to the addresses of Mr. S. I would advise you neither
to encourage or discourage his suit: for if on inquiry
into his character and circumstances, I shall find that they
are answerable to your cousin's good opinion of them and
his own assurances, I know not but his suit may be wor-

thy of attention. However, my dear girl, consider that men are deceitful, and always put the best side outwards. It may possibly, on the strict inquiry which the nature and importance of the case demands, come out far otherwise than it at present appears. Let me, therefore, advise you to act in this matter with great prudence, and that you make not yourself too cheap, for men are apt to slight what is too easily obtained. In the mean time he may be told, that you are entirely resolved to abide by my determination in an affair of this great importance. This will put him on applying to me, who, you need not doubt, will in this case, as in all others, study your good. Your mother gives her blessing to you, and joins in the advice you here receive from

Your affectionate father.

LETTER 36.

From Mr. S. to the Young Lady's Father.

Sir,

Though personally unknown to you, I take the liberty to declare the great value and affection I have for your amiable daughter, whom I have had the honor to see at my friend's house. I should think myself entirely unworthy of her favor and of your approbation, if I could have thought of influencing her resolution, but in obedience to your pleasure, as I should, on such a supposition, offer an injury likewise to that prudence in herself which I flatter myself is not the least of her amiable perfections. If I might have the honor of your countenance, sir, on

this occasion, I would open myself and circumstances to
you in that frank and honest manner, which should convince you of the sincerity of my affection for your daughter, and at the same time of the honorableness of my
intentions. In the mean time I will in general say, that
I have been set up in my business upwards of three years;
that 1 have a very good trade for the time; and that I had
a thousand dollars to begin with, which I have improved
to fifteen hundred, as I am ready to make appear to your
satisfaction ; that I am descended of a creditable family,
have done nothing to stain my character, and that my
trade is still further improvable, as I shall, I hope, enlarge
my capital. This, sir, I thought but honest and fair to
acquaint you with, that you might know something of a
person who sues you for your countenance, and that of
your good lady, in an affair that I hope may one day
prove the greatest happiness of my life, as it must be, if
I can be blessed with that and your daughter's approbation. In hope of which, and the favor of a line, I take
the liberty to subscribe myself, good sir,

Your-obedient and humble servant.

LETTER 37

*From a Young Lady to a Gentleman, complaining of Indiffer-
ence.*

Sir,

However light you may make of premises, yet I am
foolish enough to consider them as something more than

trifles ; and am likewise induced to believe that the man who voluntarily breaks a promise, will not pay much regard to an oath ; and if so, in what light must I consider your conduct? Did I not give you my promise to be yours, and had you no other cause for soliciting it than merely to gratify your vanity? A brutal gratification indeed, to triumph over the weakness of a woman, whose greatest fault was, that she loved you! I say *loved* you ; for it was in consequence of that passion, I first consented to become yours. Has your conduct, sir, been consistent with my submission, or with your own solemn professions? Is it consistent with the character of a gentleman, first to obtain a woman's consent, and afterwards brag that he had discarded her, and found one more agreeable to his wishes? Do not equivocate ; I have too convincing proofs of your insincerity ; I saw you yesterday walking with Miss B., and am informed that you have promised marriage to her. Whatever you may think, sir, I have a spirit of disdain, and even resentment, equal to your ingratitude, and can treat the wretch with a proper indifference, who can make so slight a matter of the most solemn promises. Miss B. may be your wife, but she will receive into her arms a purjured husband ; nor can ever the superstructure be lasting, which is built on such a foundation. I leave you to the stings of your own conscience.

I am, the injured.

LETTER 38.

The Gentleman's Answer.

My DEAR GIRL,

For by that name I must still call you ; has cruelty entered into your tender nature, or has some designing wretch imposed on your credulity? My dear, I am not what you have represented; I am neither false or per-jured ; I never proposed marriage to Miss B. ; I never de-signed it: and my sole reason for walking with her was, that I had been on a visit to her brother, who you know is my attorney. And was it any fault in me to take a walk into the fields with him and his sister? Surely pre-judice itself has imposed on you by some designing person, who had private views, and private ends to answer by such baseness. But whatever may have been the cause, I am entirely innocent, and to convince you of my sincerity, beg that the day of marriage be next week. My affections never so much as wander from the dear object of my love; in you are centered all my hopes of felicity ; with you only can I be happy. Keep me not in misery one mo-ment longer, by entertaining groundless jealousies against one who loves you in a manner superior to the whole of your sex ; and I can set at defiance even malice itself. Let me beg your answer by my servant, which will make me either happy or miserable. I have sent a small parcel by the bearer, which I hope you will accept as a convinc-ing proof of my integrity, and am,

Yours for ever.

LETTER 39.

From a Gentleman to a Lady, whom he accuses of Inconstancy.

MADAM,

You will not, I presume, be surprised at a letter in the place of a visit from one who cannot but have reason to believe it may easily be as welcome as his company.

You should not suppose, if lovers have lost their sight, that their senses are all banished : and if I refuse to believe my eyes when they show me your inconstancy, you must not wonder that I cannot stop my years against the accounts of it. Pray let us understand one another properly ; for I am afraid we are deceiving ourselves all this while. Am I a person whom you esteem, whose fortune you do not despise, and whose pretensions you encourage ; or am I a troublesome coxcomb, who fancy myself particularly received by a woman who only laughs at me? If I am the latter you treat me as I deserve ; and I ought to join with you in saying I deserve it. But if it be otherwise, and you receive me as I think you do, as a person you intend to marry,—for it is best to be plain on those occasions,— pray tell me, what is the meaning of that universal coquetry in public, where every fool flatters you, and you are pleased with the meanest of them? and what can be the meaning that I am told you last night was, in particular, an hour with Mr. M., and are so wherever you meet him, if I am not in company? Both of us, madam, you cannot think of; and I should be sorry to imagine, that when I had given you my heart so entirely, I shared yours with any other man.

I have said a great deal too much to you, and yet I am tempted to say more; but I shall be silent. I beg you will answer this, and I think I have a right to expect that you do it generously and fairly. Do not mistake what is the effect of the destraction of my heart, for want of respect to you. While I write thus, I dote upon you, but I cannot bear to be deceived where all my happiness is centered.

Your most unhappy L. C.

LETTER 40.

From a Lady to a Lover, who suspects her of receiving the addresses of another. In Answer.

SIR,

Did I not make all the allowance you desire in the end of your letter, I should not answer you at all. But although I am really unhappy to find you are so, and the more to find myself to be the occasion, I can hardly impute the unkindness and incivility of your letter to the single cause you would have me. However, as I would not be suspected of any thing that should justify such treatment from you, I think it necessary to inform you, that what you have heard, has no more foundation than what you have seen; however, I wonder that others' eyes should not be so easily alarmed as yours; for instead of being blind, believe me, sir, you see more than there is. Perhaps, however, their sight may be as much sharpened by unprovoked malice, as yours by undeserved suspicion.

Whatever may be the end of this dispute, for I do not

think so light of lovers' quarrels as many do, I think it proper to inform you, that I never have thought favorably of any one but yourself: and I shall add, that if the faults of your temper, which I once little suspected, should make me fear you too much to marry, you will not see me in that state with any other, nor courted by any man in all the world.

I did not know that the gayety of my temper gave you uneasiness: and you ought to have told me of it with less severity. If I am particular in it, I am afraid it is a fault in my natural disposition; but I would have taken some pains to get the better of that, if I had known it was disagreeable to you. I ought to resent this treatment more than I do, but do not insult my weakness on that head: for a fault of that kind would want the excuse this has for my pardon; and might not be so easily overlooked, though I could wish to do it. I should say, I would not see you to-day, but you have an advocate that pleads for you much better than you do for yourself. I desire you will first look carefully over this letter, for my whole heart is in it, and then come to me.

Yours, &c.

LETTER 41.

From a rich Young Gentleman, to a beautiful Young Lady, without a fortune.

Miss S.,

It is a general reflection against the manners of the present age, that marriage is only considered as one of those methods by which avarice may be satisfied, and property increased: that neither the character nor accomplishments of the woman are much regarded, her merit being estimated by the thousands of her fortune. I acknowledge that the accusation is too true, and to that may be ascribed many unhappy matches we daily meet with; for how is it possible that those should ever have the same affection for each other, who were forced to comply with terms to which they had the utmost aversion as if they had been allowed to consult their own inclinations, and gave their hands where they had engaged their hearts. For my own part, I have been always determined to consult my own inclinations, where there is the least appearance of happiness; and having an easy independency, am not anxious about increasing it; being well convinced, that in all states the middle one is the best. I mean neither poverty nor riches; which leads me to the discovery of a passion which I have long endeavored to conceal.

The opportunities which I have had of conversing with you at Mrs. A.'s, have at last convinced me that merit and riches are far from being connected, and that a woman may have those qualifications necessary to adorn her sex, although adverse fortune has denied her money. I am sure that all those virtues necessary to make me happy in the marriage state are centered in you; and whatever objection you may have to my person, yet I hope there can be none to my character; and if you will consent to be mine, it shall be my constant study to make your life agreeable, and under the endearing character of a husband, endeavor to supply your early loss of the best of parents. I shall expect your answer as soon as possible, for I wait for it with the utmost impatience.

I am your affectionate lover.

LETTER 42,

The Young Lady's Answer.

Sir,

I received your letter yesterday, and gratitude for the generous proposal which you have made, obliges me to thank you heartily for the contents.

As I have no objection either to your person or character, you will give me leave to deal sincerely, and state those things which at present bear weight with me, and perhaps must ever remain unanswered, and hinder me from entering into that state against which I have not the least aversion.

You well know, (at least I imagine so,) that the proposal you have made to me is a secret both to your relations and friends ; and would you desire me to run precipitately into the marriage state, where 1 have the greatest reason to fear that I should be looked upon with contempt, by those whom nature had connected me with ? I should consider myself obliged to promote the happiness of my husband : and how consistent would a step of that nature be with such a resolution ? You know that I was left an orphan, and had it not been for the pious care of Mrs. A., must have been brought up in a state of servitude. You

know that I have no fortune, and were I to accept of your
offer, it would lay me under such obligations as must destroy my liberty. Gratitude and love are two very different things. The one supposes a benefit received, whereas
the other is a free act of the will. Suppose me raised to
the joint possession of your fortune, could I call it mine
unless I had brought you something as an equivalent? or,
have I not great reason to fear that you yourself may consider me as under obligations inconsistent with the char-
ter of a wife? I acknowledge the great generosity of
your offer, and would consider myself highly honored,
could I prevail with myself to prefer to peace of mind the
enjoyment of an affluent fortune. But as I have been
very sincere in my answer, so let me beg, that you will
endeavor to eradicate a passion, which, if nourished longer,
may prove fatal to us both.

   I am, sir,
    With the greatest respect, &c.

      ## LETTER 43.

     The Gentleman's Reply.

DEAR S.,
  Was it not cruel to start so many objections? or could
you suppose me capable of so base an action, as to destroy
your freedom and peace of mind? or do you think that I
am capable of ever forgetting you, or being happy in the
enjoyment of another? For affection's sake, do not mention gratitude any more. Your many virtues entitle you
to much more than I am able to give; but all that I have

shall be yours. With respect to my relations, I have none to consult besides my mother and uncle, and their consent, and even approbation, are already obtained. You have often heard my mother declare, that she preferred my happiness with a woman of virtue, to the possession of the greatest fortune; and though I forgot to mention it, yet I had communicated my sentiments to her before I had opened my mind to you. Let me beg that you will lay aside all those unnecessary scruples, which only serve to make one unhappy who is already struggling under all the anxieties of real and genuine love. It is in your power, my dear, to make me happy, and none else can. I cannot enjoy one moment's rest till I have your answer, and then the happy day shall be fixed. Let me beg that you will not start any more objections, unless you are my real enemy; but your tender nature cannot suffer you to be cruel. Be mine, my dear, and I am yours forever. My servant shall wait for the answer to your ever sincere lover, whose whole happiness is centered in you.

I am, &c.

LETTER 44.

The Lady's Answer.

Sir,

I find that, like most of your sex, when you have formed a resolution, you are determined to go through with it, whatever be the event. Your answer to my first objection, I must confess, is satisfactory. I wish I could

say so of the others; but I find if I must comply, I shall
be obliged to trust the remainder to yourself. Perhaps
this is always the case, and even the most cautious have
been deceived. However, sir, I have communicated the
contents of your letter to Mrs. A., as you know she has
been to me as a parent. She has not any objection, and
I am at last resolved to comply. I must give myself up
to you as a poor, friendless orphan, and shall endeavor to
act consistent with the rules laid down and enforced by
our holy religion: and if you should so far deviate from
the paths of virtue as to upbraid me with poverty, I have
no friend to complain to but God, who is the *father of the
fatherless.* But I have a better opinion of you than to
entertain any such fears. I have left the time to your
own appointment; and let me beg that you will continue
in the practice of that virtuous education which you have
received. Virtue is its own reward, and I cannot be unhappy with the man who prefers the duties of religion to
gayety and dissipation.

I am yours sincerely.

ON RELATIONSHIP.

— —

LETTER 45.

From a Young Lady to her Mother.

Give me leave, my dear mother, to tell you, as well as my pen will permit me, or rather as well as my inexperienced hand is capable of directing it, how truly sensible I am of all your favors, and that I will endeavor by my conduct to merit the continuance of them. My prayers are, morning and night, offered up to heaven for your preservation, nor are you ever in the day absent from my thoughts. May Providence preserve you, and grant you every thing you can wish for, from the good behavior of

Your dutiful and affectionate daughter.

———

LETTER 46.

From a Young Lady to her Brother in the Country.

You seem, my dear Bill, to make good the old proverb, "Out of sight, out of mind." It is now two months since I received a letter from you, and you appear to forget that we little maids do not like to be treated with neglect. You must not pretend to tell me, that however fond you may be of your books, you could not find leisure to write me

in all this time. They tell me that you spend a great
part of your leisure time with a little Miss of about eight
years of age, with whom you are very fond of reading
and conversing. Take care, if I find she is withdrawing
your affection from me, that I do not come down and pull
her cap for her. As for yourself, if you were within the
reach of my little tongue, I would give you such a peal as
should make you remember it for some time to come.
However, if you will write to me soon, I may possibly forgive all that is past, and still consider myself as

Your most affectionate sister.

LETTER 47.

Answer to the preceding.

I am very sorry, my dear sister, that I have given
you so much reason to complain of my neglect of writing
to you; but be assured, that my affections for you are the
same they ever were. I readily confess, that the young
lady you complain of has in some measure been the cause
of it. She is as fond of reading as I am, and I believe
loves you on my account; is it then possible my sister can
be displeased with one so amiable? I did not tell her
what you threatened her with : but I am sure, were you
to come here on that errand, instead of pulling her cap,
you would embrace and love her. As to what you say
respecting your little tongue, I promise you I do not wish
to come within reach of the sound of it, when anger sets
it in motion. As this is the only thing which can render

my sister less agreeable, I shall be very cautious to avoid setting the little alarum in motion, especially when I shall pay you a visit. I have bought you a most brilliant doll, which I shall bring up with me when I come to Hudson. Till then, believe me

Your most affectionate brother.

LETTER 48.

From a Brother to a Sister in the country, upbraiding her for being negligent in writing.

MY DEAR SISTER,

I write to you to acquaint you how unkindly we all take it here, that you do not write oftener to us, in relation to your health, diversion, and employments in the country. You cannot be insensible how much you are beloved by us all; judge then if you do well to omit giving us the satisfaction absence affords to true friends, which is often to hear from one another. My mother is highly disobliged with you, and says you are a very idle girl; my aunt is of the same opinion, and I would fain, like a loving brother, excuse you if I could. Pray, for the future, take care to deserve a better character, and by writing soon, and often, put it in my power to say what a good sister I have: For you shall always find me,

Your most affectionate brother.

4

LETTER 49.

From the Daughter to the Mother, in excuse for the neglect.

MY DEAR MOTHER,

I am ashamed I stayed to be reminded of my duty by my brother's kind letter. I will offer no excuse for myself, for not writing oftener, though I have been strangely taken up by the kindness and favor of your good friends here, particularly my aunt, for well do I know that my duty to my honored mother ought to take place of all other considerations. All I beg, therefore, is, that you will be so good as to forgive me, on promise of amendment. Believe me when I say that no diversions here or elsewhere shall make me forget the duty I owe to so good a mother, and such kind relations ; and that I shall ever be

Your gratefully dutiful daughter.

P. S. My aunt and cousins desire their kind love to you, and respects to all friends.

LETTER 50.

From a Father to his Son at School.

I could not, my dear child, give a more convincing proof of my affection for you, than in submitting to send you to so great a distance from me. I preferred your advantage to my own pleasure, and sacrificed fondness to duty. I should have done this sooner, but I waited until my inquiries had found out a person whose character might be responsible for your education ; and Mr. B. was at length my choice for that important trust. Your obedience, therefore, must be without murmuring or reluctance; especially when you reflect that a strict attention to his appointments, and an implicit compliance with his commands, are not only to form the rule of your safe conduct in this life, but to be preparatory to your happiness in the next. With regard to your school connections, it is impossible for me to give you any instructions at present. All that I shall now say to you on this subject is, quarrel with no one, avoid meddling with the disputes of others, unless with a view to promote an accommodation; and though I would wish you to support the dignity of a youth, be neither mean nor arrogant. I have nothing more now to add, than to pray to God to give you grace and abilities, and that your own endeavors may second the views of

An affectionate father.

LETTER 51.

From a Youth at school to his Father.

I am infinitely obliged to you, honored sir, for the many favors you have bestowed upon me; all I hope is, that the progress I make in my learning will be considered as some proof how sensible I am of your kindness. Gratitude, duty, and a view to my own future advantage, equally contribute to make me thoroughly sensible how much I ought to labor for my own improvement and your satisfaction. I have received the books you sent for my amusement. They please me much. The liberal allowance of money you have been pleased to make to me, shall be applied in the best manner I am able. I am sure my dear father will not censure me, should I devote a part of it towards the relief of the wretched and unfortunate. Pray give my most dutiful respects to my mother, my kindest love to my brothers and sisters, and believe me, dear sir,

Your most dutiful,
And affectionate son.

LETTER 52.

From an elder Brother to a Younger one at school.

As you are now, my dear brother, gone from home, and placed in a very capital seminary of learning, I thought it not amiss to put you in mind, that childish amusements should be laid aside, and, instead of them, more serious thoughts imbibed, and things of more consequence made the objects of your attention ; whereby we may add to the reputation of our family, and gain to ourselves the good esteem of being virtuous and diligent. You may judge, in some measure, of the value of a good education, from the unavailing lamentations you daily hear those make, who have foolishly shrunk from the difficulties attending the various branches of scholastic education. What a difference there is between an aged man of learning, and one who totally neglected his education in his youth ! The former, in the evening of his life, finds a perpetual source of amusement in the knowledge he has acquired in his early days, and his company is admired and sought by all those who wish to derive understanding from the knowledge of others, improved by a long life and philosophical experience; but the ignorant old man is no company for himself, nor any one else, unless over a pitcher or a bottle, when the assistance of a pipe will be necessary to excuse his silence. I know you have too much good nature to be offended at my advice, especially when I assure you, that I as sincerely wish your happiness and advancement in life as I do my own. We are all very well, thank God, and your friends desire to be remembered to you. Pray write as often as opportunity and leisure will permit; and be assured that a letter from you will always give great satisfaction to your parents, but to none more than to your most

Affectionate brother.

LETTER 53.

From an Uncle to a Nephew, on his keeping bad company, bad hours, &c.

DEAR NEPHEW,

I am very much concerned to hear, that you are of late fallen into bad company; that you keep late hours; and have entered into clubs and societies of young fellows, who set at naught all good example, and make such persons who would do their duty the subject of their ridicule, as persons of narrow minds, and who want the courage to do as they do.

Consider, I exhort you, in time, to what these courses may lead you. Consider the affliction you will give to all your friends by your continuance in them. Lay together the substance of the conversation that passes in a whole evening, with your frothy companions, after you have come from them, and reflect what solid truth, what useful lessons, worthy of being inculcated in your future life, that whole evening has afforded you; and consider whether it is worth breaking through all rule and order for. Whether you are so capable to pursue your business with that ardor and delight next morning, as if you had not drank or kept bad hours over night. Whether the taking of small liberties, as you may think them, leads you on to greater. For let me tell you, you will not find it in your power to stop when you will: and then, whether any restraint at all will not in time be irksome to you.

You are now at an age, when you should study to improve, not divert your faculties. You should now lay in a fund of knowledge, that in time, when ripened by experience, may make you a worthier member of the commonwealth. Do you think you have nothing to learn, either as to your business, or as to the forming of your mind? Would it not be much better to choose the silent, the sober conversation of books, than of such companions as never read or think? An author seldom commits any but his best thoughts to paper; but what can you expect from the laughing, noisy company you keep, but frothy prate, indigested notions, and thoughts so unworthy of being remembered that it is the greatest wisdom to forget them?

Let me entreat you then, my dear kinsman, for your family's sake, for your own sake, before it be too late, to reflect as you ought upon the course you have entered into. By applying yourself to books instead of such vain company, you will be qualified in time for the best of company, and be respected by all ranks of men. This will keep you out of unnecessary expenses, will employ all your leisure time, will exclude a world of temptations, and finally set you above that wretched company which now you seem so much delighted with. And one thing let me recommend to you, that you keep a list of the young men of your standing within the compass of your knowledge, and for a few years observe what fate will attend them; see if those who follow not the course you have so lately entered into, will not appear in a very different light from those who do: and for the industry and prosperity of the one, and the decay or failure of the other, (if their vain ways do not blast them before or as soon as they begin the world,) you'll find abundant reason every day to justify the truth of the observations I have thrown together. As nothing but my affection for you could possibly influence me to these expostulations, I hope for a proper effect from them, if you would be thought well of by, or expect any favor from,

Your loving uncle.

LETTER 54.

An Uncle in answer to a Nephew's complaining of hardships in his Apprenticeship.

DEAR NEPHEW,

I am sorry you should have any misunderstanding with your master: I have a good opinion of him and am unwilling to entertain a bad one of you. It is so much a master's interest to use his apprentices well, that I am disposed to think, that when they are badly used, it is oftener the effect of provocation than choice. Wherefore, before I give myself the trouble of interposing in your behalf, I desire you will strictly inquire of yourself, whether you have not, by some misconduct or other, provoked that alteration in your master's behaviour of which you so much complain. If, after having diligently complied with this request, you assure me that you are not sensible of having given cause of disgust on your side, I will readily use my endeavors to reconcile you to your master, or procure you another. But if you find yourself blamable, it will be better for you to remove, by your own amendment, the occasion of your master's displeasure, than to have me, or any other friend, offer to plead your excuse, where you know it would be unjust to defen you. If this should be your ease, all your friends together could promise your better behavior, indeed; but as the performance must even then be your own, it will add much more to your character to pass through your whole term, without any interposition between you. Weigh what I have here said; and rememher that your future welfare depends greatly on your present behavior.

I am your loving kinsman.

LETTER 55.

From a Young Man, who had eloped from his Apprenticeship, to his Father, desiring him to intercede with his Master to take him again into his service.

Honored Sir,

With shame, arising from a consciousness of guilt, I have presumed to write to you at this time. I doubt not but you have heard of the irregularities in my conduct, which at last proceeded so far, as to induce me to desert the service of the best of masters. Filled with the deepest contrition, and sensible of my folly and ingratitude, I know not of a more powerful advocate to intercede for me, than my honored, though justly offended parent. It was the allurements of vicious company that first tempted me to forsake the path of virtue, and neglect my duty in a family, where I was treated with the greatest tenderness. Fully sensible of my fault, I am willing to make every reparation in my power; but know not of any other than by acting diametrically opposite to my former conduct. Let me entreat you to intercede with my worthy master to take me again into his service, and my whole future life shall be one continued act of gratitude.

I am, sir, your affectionate,
Though undutiful son.

LETTER 56.

To a Friend on his Recovery from a dangerous illness.

DEAR SIR,

Give me leave to mingle my joy with that of all your friends and relations, in the recovery of your health, and to join with them to bless God for continuing to your numerous well-wishers, the benefit of your useful and valuable life. That he may long preserve you in health, and prosper all your undertakings, for the good of your worthy family, and the pleasure of all your friends and acquaintances, is the hearty prayer of, sir,

Your faithful friend,

And humble servant.

LETTER 57.

An Answer to the Preceding.

DEAR SIR,

I give you many thanks for your kind congratulations. My return of health will be the greater pleasure to me, if I can contribute in any measure to the happiness of my good friends ; and particularly to that of you and yours : for I assure you, sir, that nobody can be more than I am,

Your obliged humble servant.

LETTER 58.

From a Young Gentleman to his afflicted Friend.

I cannot fail, my dear Harry, most sensibly to feel the loss you have sustained in the death of a good and indulgent father. It pierces me to the heart: for I know how great was your affection for him, and how you must feel his loss. I will call upon you to-morrow, and we will mourn together; for, as we always mutually enjoyed our sports, why should we be separated in our griefs? They tell me you do not cry, but sit in gloomy silence. I do not like this; for I have somewhere read, that tears ease the heart, and open a passage for the anguish of the soul. That Heaven may give you patience under this terrible calamity, is the most fervent prayer of

Your disconsolate friend.

LETTER 59.

Answer to the preceding.

I know of nothing in this world but a letter from my dear friend, that could have so soon awakened me from the deep and melancholy gloom with which I was overwhelmed. Your letter forced from my eyes a flood of tears, and since that my heart is much easier. Am I not wicked in thus repining at my hard fate, when it is undoubtedly the work, the pleasure of that great Being, to whose will, my dear father has often told me, we ought at all times to submit? Others, perhaps better children than myself, have experienced the like loss, and more submit to the same dreadful misfortune. My poor mother is almost distracted, and my grief, I perceive, adds to hers. I will, therefore, endeavor to conceal it. Let me see you to-day or to-morrow at farthest; which is all I can say at present, but—what a father have I lost!

LETTER 60.

To a Father, concerning the choice of a proper profession for his Son.

DEAR SIR,

You very well know that I have a good opinion of your son, and think him a modest, grave and sober youth. For this reason, I hardly think him qualified for the profession you seem inclined to choose for him; for I much doubt whether he has talents for the law, or ever will have that presence of mind which is indispensably necessary, in order to make a figure at the bar. In any smooth and easy business he will probably succeed, and be a useful member of the community. I must confess to you, and I hope you will excuse the freedom, that I have some doubts whether your son's genius may be equal to that of a universal merchant. This opinion, which I have entertained of your son, should you think it just, will be no obstacle to his succeeding in the world, in some creditable and easy business. Though I think him unequal to the profession you seem disposed to allot him, yet I by no means think him destitute of common sense: and experience teaches us, that in some sort of business, ample advantages may be made by very moderate talents, with much reputation. These are principally such employments as merely consist in buying with prudence, and in selling goods at a profit. Hence we see several wholesale dealers gain large fortunes with ease and credit, and without any other secret, than the plain practice of buying at the best hand, paying for their goods punctually, and vending them always for what they really are. As to what you hint of placing him in the physical tribe, I like that no better than the other. Consider only this one thing, how long it will be before he will be capable of entering into business, or acquiring reputation as a physician, if he ever does it at all; for who chooses to trust his health to an inexperienced young man? The lawyer needs a sprightly impudence, if I may so say, and the physician a solemn one. It is from hence easy to foresee, that he may, in the profession of either physic or law, live over all his days, and remain at last quite unknown; for as practice in both faculties is the best teacher, and theory a most certain guide, he may live to forty or fifty years of age, and not come into any business that shall improve himself, or benefit his consulters. Whereas, in the way I propose, no sooner shall he become of age, and fit to be trusted with the management of any affairs at all, but his seven years will be expired.; and if he has not been inattentive to his business, he will be enabled, with the fortune you can bestow upon him, to enter on the stage of the world with great advantage, and become directly a necessary and useful member of the

community. My good friend, when you and I recollect
that most of the best families in this country, as well as
the genteel ones, had the foundation of their grandeur laid
in trade, I expect not in such a country as ours especially,
that any objection to my advice will be formed, either by
you or your lady on this score, if you have not more sig-
nificant reasons, proceeding from the youth's turn of
mind and inclination, which, I think, should always be
consulted on these occasions. By thus viewing your son
in the same light I do, that of a well inclined lad, of
moderate passions, great natural modesty, and no soaring
genius, I believe you will think it best to dispose of him
in such a manner as may require no greater talents than
he is possessed of, and may in due time make him appear,
in the face of the world, fully qualified for what he under-
takes.

I am sir, &c.

———

LETTER 61.

From one Friend to another in distress, with offers of assistance.

DEAR SIR,

The great losses you have sustained by the failure of
Mr. R., have caused me much uneasiness. I hope you
behave under it like the man of prudence you have
always shown yourself. As one who knows how liable all
men are to misfortunes, I think it is incumbent, on this
occasion, not to console you by words only, but, with the
spirit and cheerfulness of a sincere friend, to offer you my

service, to answer any present demand, so far as two hundred dollars will go. This you shall freely have the use of for a twelve-month, or more, if your affairs require it; and I will even strain a point, rather than not oblige you, if more be necessary to your present situation. You will do me great pleasure in accepting this offer as freely as it is kindly meant by,

Dear sir, yours most faithfully,

LETTER 62.

An Answer to the preceding offer.

MY DEAR FRIEND,

The grateful sense I have of your kindness will never be erased from my mind. This is, indeed, an instance of true friendship! I accept, most thankfully, of some part of your generous offer, and I will give you my note, payable in a year, for one hundred dollars. This is at present all that I have occasion for; and if I did not know I could then, if not before, answer your goodness as it deserves, I would not accept of the favor. This loss is very heavy and affecting to me, as you may suppose; yet your generous friendship is no small comfort to me in it. So good a friend is capable of making any calamity light.

I am, dear sir,

Your faithful and obliged servant.

CARDS OF COMPLIMENT.

Mr. and Mrs. Cecil's compliments to Mr. and Mrs. Howard, and desire the favor of their company on Wednesday next, to take tea and spend the evening.
Monday Morning.

Mr. and Mrs. Howard return their compliments to Mr. and Mrs. Cecil, and will certainly do themselves the pleasure to accept their polite invitation.
Monday Noon.

Mr. and Mrs. Howard return their compliments, and are sorry that a pre-engagement will not permit them the pleasure of waiting on Mr. and Mrs. Cecil, which they would have otherwise readily done.
Monday Morning.

Mr. and Mrs. Compton's compliments to Mr. and Mrs. Stanley; and if they are disengaged this afternoon, will take the pleasure of waiting on them.
Tuesday Morning.

Mr. and Mrs. Stanley are perfectly disengaged, beg their compliments, and will be extremely glad of Mr. and Mrs. Compton's agreeable company.
Tuesday Noon.